WHALE DONE,
MY WONDERFUL ONE!

KEN BLANCHARD
Coauthor of *The One Minute Manager*®

Sue Zlatin and Cathy Huett • Illustrations by Jane R. Griffith

WILLIAM MORROW
An Imprint of HarperCollins*Publishers*

To Alec, my wonderful grandson,
who makes me laugh and love life.
-Ken

To my wonderful grandchildren,
Mason and Decker,
our family's Whale Done legacy!
-Sue

To Dawn, my wonderful one, a daughter
who increasingly inspires me.
-Cathy

ABOUT THE *WHALE DONE!* PHILOSOPHY

For years I've been telling business leaders that the key to developing people is to catch them doing things right. Yet I still find that people know they're doing a good job only when nobody's yelled at them lately. Sadly, this "leave alone/zap" leadership style is not only practiced by managers but by parents, grandparents, and teachers as well.

I have always believed that punishment is harmful in human relationships. When I saw my first killer whale show in San Diego—where the most feared predators in the ocean had been trained to leap, dive, and do all kinds of tricks on command—I was fascinated. Did the trainers punish the whales when they did something wrong and then get back in the water with them? Common sense tells you this wouldn't be a smart move. During a behind the scenes tour of SeaWorld®, I learned that when a whale shows undesirable behavior, the trainers do not punish it. Instead, they redirect its energies back on what it was supposed to do and praise the whale when it behaves appropriately.

Inspired by this great example, I teamed up with SeaWorld's head whale trainer Chuck Tompkins, his long time colleague Thad Lacinak, and my good friend Jim Ballard to write the best selling *Whale Done! The Power of Positive Relationships*. If the simple tools of building trust, accentuating the positive, and redirecting could get five-ton whales to jump thirty feet in the air, we knew they would work with people as well. We also knew if it worked for whales and grownups, it would be good for kids, which led us to write *Whale Done Parenting*.

Whale Done, My Wonderful One! is a fun story for kids that illustrates what Sue Zlatin, Cathy Huett, and I have found to be true: **Effective parenting is not something you do *to* children; it's something you do *with* them.**

The young whale in this story gets himself in the worst circumstances, but even so his mother is an understanding and caring parent. You can be, too, when you build your kids' trust, praise them, and redirect their mistakes to keep them safe and bring out their best. That's the way to create a loving partnership. Whether you're a parent, grandparent, relative, teacher, or friend, I invite you to use this book to grow with the children in your life and create loving, trusting relationships.

—Ken Blanchard

COAUTHOR, *THE ONE MINUTE MANAGER®* AND *LEADING AT A HIGHER LEVEL*

Good morning, Sun
As you rise for the day,
You greet us in the warmest way.
Whale done, my wonderful Sun!

"Good Morning, Dale!" said Mother Whale,
Tickling her calf with her rubbery tail.
"Good Morning, Mom! Can we go play?"
"Sure!" said his mom. "We'll start right away!"

His mom said proudly, "Swim this way!
What do you want to do *whale* today?
You're a good listener—and swimmer, too.
Just follow me now. I will teach you!"

"We'll dive deep down where the water is black.
Don't be afraid—we'll come right back.
When we're done exploring there
I'll show you how to surface for air."

"Okay, Mom! I'll do what you say.
Diving is what I'll do *whale* today!"
They turned out to sea and swam for a while.
"Let's dive here!" said Mom with a smile.

Mom was pleased with his diving skill.
"You're doing *whale*, and for that I'm thrilled!
We'll go up for air when our dive is done.
Whale done, my wonderful one!"

"Mom," said Dale as they swam through the sea,
"Why do you say 'Whale done' to me?"
"Because," Mom said, "when we try something new,
Praise helps us learn what we're trying to do."

"I like praise," said Dale. "It makes me feel good—
Like I can do everything just as I should."
Mom said, "You can do all you set your heart to.
You're a fine young whale. I believe in you."

Dale thought he was ready to dive alone,
So he turned away and started to roam.
Swimming far from his mom, he went off to play,
Till he saw a huge shark heading his way!

He swam fast to escape, but before too long
He knew he had done something terribly wrong.
A strong current caught him and swirled him away.
He couldn't get free of it, try as he may!

Tumbling and turning, he finally hit land
Above the cool sea on a ridge made of sand.
He called for his mom with a loud clicking sound,
But out of the sea this was useless, he found!

Dale's mom called out and her call echoed back.
She hoped that she was on the right track.
Swimming toward land, she saw from afar
Her sweet little whale stuck on the sandbar!

So she swam very fast with her powerful tail.
She reached the sandbar and a very scared Dale.
She wiggled and rocked in a gentle motion
Until they were both back in the ocean.

Dale's mom was wise and knew he was learning.
She knew not to yell or punish his yearnings.
"I made a mistake, Mom, and did something bad.
Why didn't you yell? Why aren't you mad?"

"Because," she replied, "when a whale goes off track,
You don't punish or scold; you help him get back.
You cheer a whale on when he does well,
When he makes a mistake, you sure don't yell.

"You show him again how things should be done,
Then say, 'Whale done, my wonderful one!'"
"I'm sorry," said Dale, "that I swam out of sight.
I'm so glad I'm here with you tonight."

She told him she loved him, and in the Whale Done way,
Praised him for what he'd done *whale* that day.
With the starry sky's moon shining above,
Dale felt safe to be home, wrapped in Mom's love.

"Tomorrow we'll try it again," Mom said,
Snuggling up close and rubbing Dale's head.
She knew their adventures had just begun.
"I love you, my wonderful one! Whale Done!"